LION IN THE LONG GRASS

for Charlie

Text Copyright © 2002 by Ruth Brown. Illustrations copyright © 2002 by Ken Brown.
This paperback edition first published in 2004 by Andersen Press Ltd.
The rights of Ruth and Ken Brown to be identified as the author and illustrator of this work has been asserted
by them in accordance with the Copyright, Designs and Patents Act, 1988. First published in Great Britain in 2002
by Andersen Press Ltd., 20 Vauxhall Bridge Road, London SW1V 2SA. Published in Australia by
Random House Australia Pty., 20 Alfred Street, Milsons Point, Sydney, NSW 2061.
All rights reserved. Colour separated in Switzerland by Photolitho, Zürich.
Printed and bound in Italy by Grafiche AZ, Verona.

10 9 8 7 6 5 4 3

British Library Cataloguing in Publication Data available.

ISBN 978 1 84270 339 7

This book has been printed on acid-free paper

LION IN THE LONG GRASS

Written by Ruth Brown
Pictures by Ken Brown

Andersen Press
London

It was early in the morning and the lioness was hungry. But before she went hunting she hid her cub in the long grass.

Lion Cub was all alone . . . or so he thought.
He couldn't see the pack of jackals circling him in the
distance. They couldn't see him either, but they knew he was
there, for they had watched while his mother had hidden him.
The jackals crept closer and closer.

Suddenly Lion Cub heard rustling in the long grass. He looked up and came face to face, not with a jackal, but with a huge lion.

Old Lion had wondered what the scavenging jackals were after. Now he knew. But they wouldn't dare come any closer. He might be old and doddery but he was still a match for a few mangy jackals.

Bravely, Lion Cub waddled forward and nuzzled the old lion's whiskery chin.

The smell of the cub was warm and familiar. It reminded Old Lion of a time long, long ago when he was young and strong and the leader of the pride.

But that was then and things were different now. Now he was old and thin, and very, very tired. Now, all he wanted to do was sleep.

Old Lion lay down in the shade of a tree.

Lion Cub followed and settled himself between Old Lion's huge, rough paws. He felt warm and safe.

Soon, the sun was high in the sky and the insects were buzzing.

Lion Cub woke up and swatted the flies on Old Lion's nose. But Old Lion didn't stir.

Lion Cub tickled Old Lion's whiskers. But Old Lion went on sleeping.

Lion Cub climbed up and chewed Old Lion's ear.
But still Old Lion didn't wake up.

So Lion Cub pounced
on Old Lion's tail and
bit it.
   This time Old Lion
did wake up.
   He growled a low
threatening growl
that got louder and
louder until it turned
into a ROAR.

Shocked, Lion Cub dashed behind the tree.
    But Old Lion didn't want to chase him. He had
been wakened by the scent of a new danger:
on the other side of the clearing stood
a large, young, snarling lion.
    Lion Cub watched, trembling,
as the two lions circled round
and round, growling and
pawing the ground.

Suddenly the young lion saw his chance and lunged, catching Old Lion with a vicious blow to the side of the neck.

Old Lion staggered, but as his head went down he saw the frightened cub. If he failed now, it would be defenceless. With one last mighty effort, Old Lion gathered his strength . . .

. . . and flung himself at the intruder. The young lion fell to the ground. Old Lion was the master now.

The young lion knew he was beaten. He ducked to avoid
Old Lion's slashing claws and fled into the safety of the
long grass.

Old Lion was exhausted but he knew the cub would be safe now. He slumped back onto his haunches and tried to catch his breath.

Slowly he sank to the ground. Lion Cub crept out
from behind the tree and gently nuzzled the whiskery
old chin. Then he settled down again between Old Lion's
huge paws and waited . . .

In the evening the lioness returned. She ran into the clearing, then stopped. Her hackles rose at the sight of the old lion, and she started to growl. Lion Cub woke up, but Old Lion didn't stir.

The lioness called softly to her cub and he ran to greet her.

Then Lion Cub turned and looked back. He roared
a quiet little roar, but Old Lion lay perfectly still
in the long grass.